Published in USA, 2023
Printed in Canada by Friesens Corporation

Library of Congress Control Number: ISBN 978-1-7362093-2-5

Dedicated to

all the living things that share our planet.

The
Seeking
Tree

There once was a sapling who wanted nothing more than to commune with everything in its magical world.

Deer, birds, bears, foxes, and even insects would sit with the trees.

But there was one part of its world that wouldn't...

Will you sit with us?

They are busy, Small One.
They work to hunt and gather.

Will you sit with us?

They are busy, Small One.
They travel to find community.

But they have hunted
and gathered.

Now, they travel to
find community?

When will they sit with us?

8

Will you sit with us?

They are busy, Young One.
They build shelters for comfort.

But they have hunted
and gathered.

They have found
community.

Now, they build
shelters for comfort?

When will they sit with us?

Will you sit with us?

13

They are busy, Young One.
They build roads to connect
with others.

14

But they have hunted and gathered.

They have found community.

They have built shelters for comfort.

Now, they build roads to connect with others?

When will they sit with us?

They are busy, Young One.
They are fighting for freedom.

18

But they have hunted
and gathered.

They have found
community.

They have built
shelters for comfort.

They have built roads
to connect with others.

Now, they fight
for freedom?

When will they sit with us?

Will you sit with us?

They are busy, Young One.
They mass produce food
for sustenance.

20

But they have hunted
and gathered.

They have found
community.

They have built
shelters for comfort.

They have built roads
to connect with others.

They have fought
for freedom.

Now, they mass produce
food for sustenance?

When will they sit with us?

They are busy, Grown One.
They use machines to move
and do things faster.

But they have hunted
and gathered.

They have found
community.

They have built
shelters for comfort.

They have built roads
to connect with others.

They have fought
for freedom.

They have mass produced
food for sustenance.

Now, they use machines to
move and do things faster.

When will they sit with us?

Will you sit with us?

11 : 11 : 01 : 03
02-21-2344

27

For thousand of years
we have watched.

They have found
community.

They have built
shelters for comfort.

They have built roads
to connect with others.

They have fought
for freedom.

They have mass produced
food for sustenance.

They have used machines
to move and do things faster.

Now, all that sits with us are machines?

"Mommy, what is that?"

"That is a tree. There used to be millions of them. Most are exctinct. There are only a few left; that's one of them."

30

STRIKER HOVERBOARDS

13:09:29:11 - 10-09-3072

The future of
hovercars
is here

NAL 1

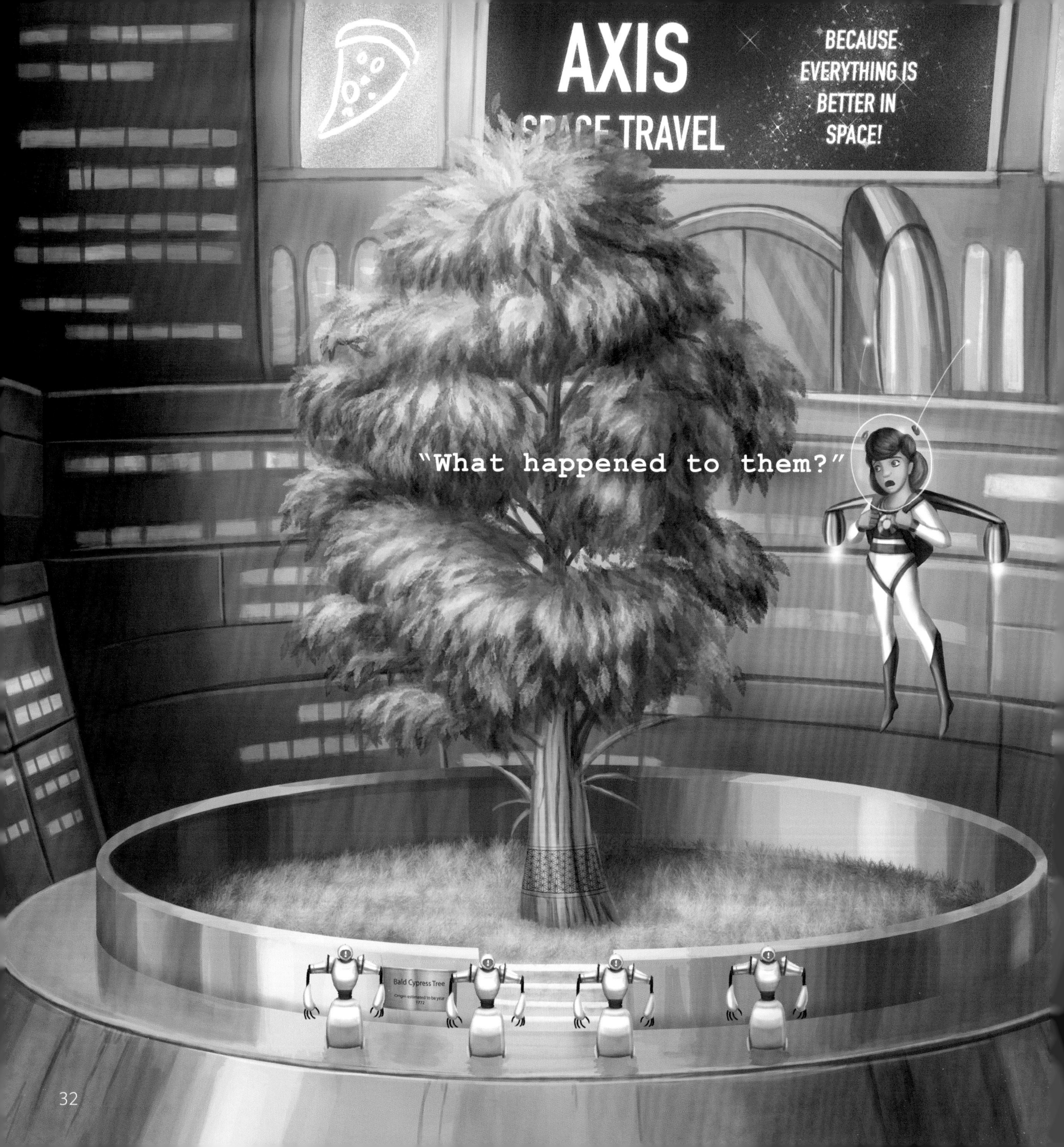

"What happened to them?"

Bald Cypress Tree

Origin estimated to be year
1772

"The world changed. There are
so many people. Some say there
wasn't enough space for them."

"WARNING! BALD CYPRESS SEED PODS ARE NOT FOR HUMAN CONSUMPTION. REPEAT. BALD CYPRESS SEED PODS ARE NOT FOR HUMAN CONSUMPTION."

"Will you help?
Can you plant one?
You can change our future!
Please protect the trees."

Will you sit with us?
Will you sit with us?
Will you sit with us?
Will you sit with us?
Will you sit with us?
Will you sit with us?
Will you sit with us?
Will you sit with us?
Will you sit with us?
Will you sit with us?
Will you sit with us?
Will you sit with us?
Will you sit with us?
Will you sit with us?
Will you sit with us?
Will you sit with us?
Will you sit with us?
Will you sit with us?
Will you sit with us?
Will you sit with us?
Will you sit with us?
Will you sit with us?

Some of the oldest living things on our planet are the majestic trees that stand beside us. Many species of trees can live for thousands of years, like the Bald cypress tree in this story!

The record holder is the ancient Great Basin bristlecone pine. It is estimated to be over 5,000 years old (and is still alive as of the writing of this book). It is one of the oldest non-clonal trees in the world, and one of the oldest living organisms on planet Earth! These trees can survive even the severest droughts, by going into a dormant state and only reawakening when the rain or snow begins to fall again.

Other record holders are the Giant sequoia, Sierra juniper, Patagonian cypress, Sacred fig, and African baobab.

Trees are an important part of our world.

ALSO BY JODI DEE

To learn more, or for free resources, coloring pages, and lesson plans visit:
jodidee.com